ANIMALS AT A G

FARM ANIMALS

For a free color catalog describing Gareth Stevens' list of high-quality books, call 1-800-542-2595 (USA) or 1-800-461-9120 (Canada). Gareth Stevens' Fax: (414) 225-0377.

The editor would like to thank Elizabeth S. Frank, Curator of Large Mammals at the Milwaukee County Zoo, Milwaukee, Wisconsin, for her kind and professional assistance regarding the accuracy of the information in this book.

Library of Congress Cataloging-in-Publication Data

Dudek, Isabella.
[Bauernhof. English]
Farm animals / by Isabella Dudek : illustrated by Heinrich Kita.
p. cm. -- (Animals at a glance)
Includes index.
ISBN 0-8368-1356-1
1. Domestic animals--Juvenile literature. [1. Domestic animals.]
I. Kita, Heinrich, ill. II. Title. III. Series: Lerne Tiere kennen.
English.
SF75.5.D8313 1995
636--dc20 95-13458

This edition first published in 1996 by
Gareth Stevens Publishing
1555 North RiverCenter Drive, Suite 201
Milwaukee, Wisconsin 53212, USA

Series editor: Barbara J. Behm
Editorial assistants: Diana L. Kahn, Diane Laska
Logo Design: Helene Feider

Printed in Mexico

1 2 3 4 5 6 7 8 9 99 98 97 96

ANIMALS AT A GLANCE

FARM ANIMALS

by ISABELLA DUDEK
Illustrated by HEINRICH KITA

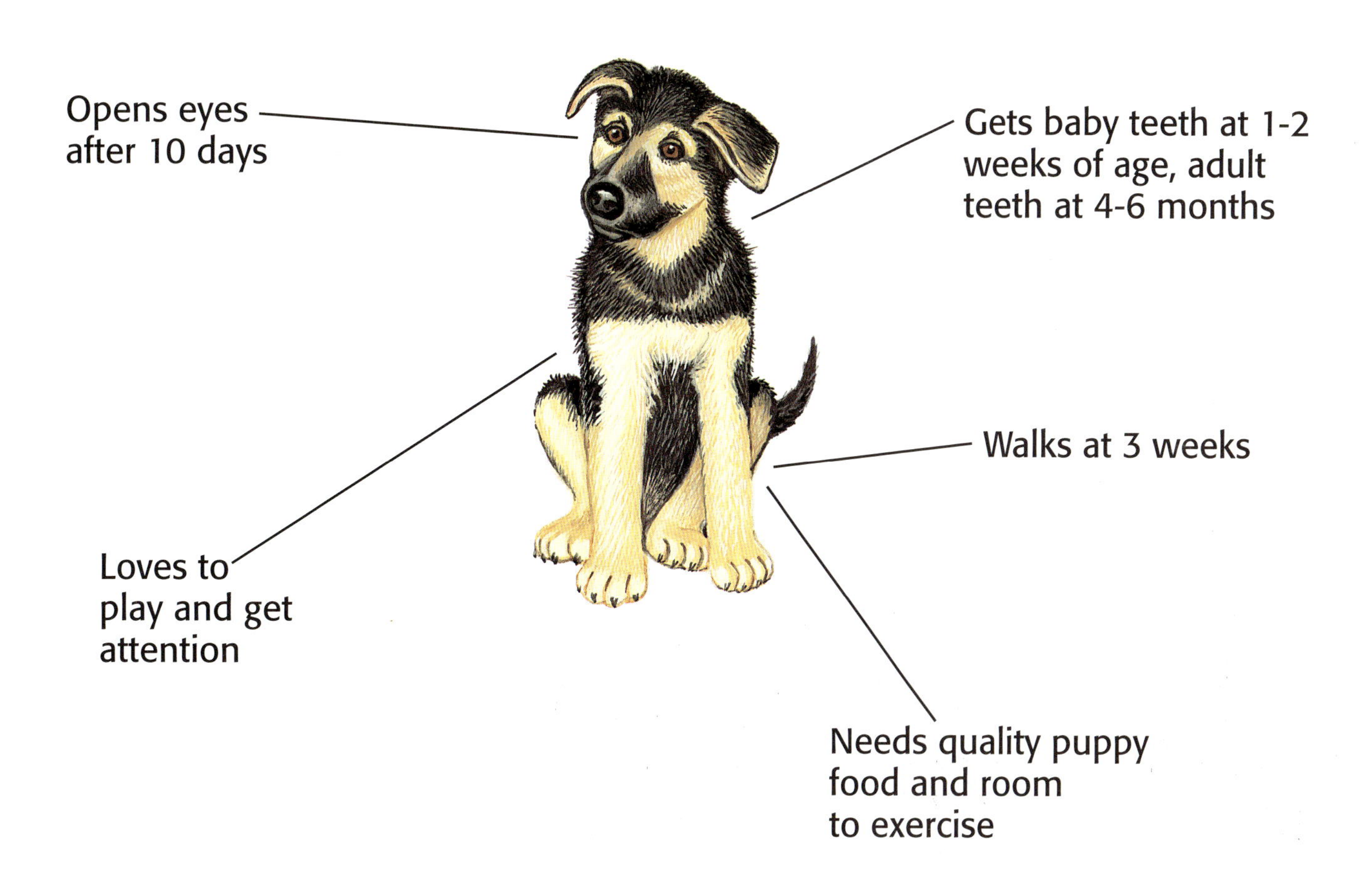
Opens eyes after 10 days
Gets baby teeth at 1-2 weeks of age, adult teeth at 4-6 months
Walks at 3 weeks
Loves to play and get attention
Needs quality puppy food and room to exercise

Gareth Stevens Publishing
MILWAUKEE

The **Horse** is a four-legged mammal. It has existed for sixty million years. It was tamed about 3000 B.C.

The **Belgian draft horse** first came from Belgium. It is a large, strong horse.

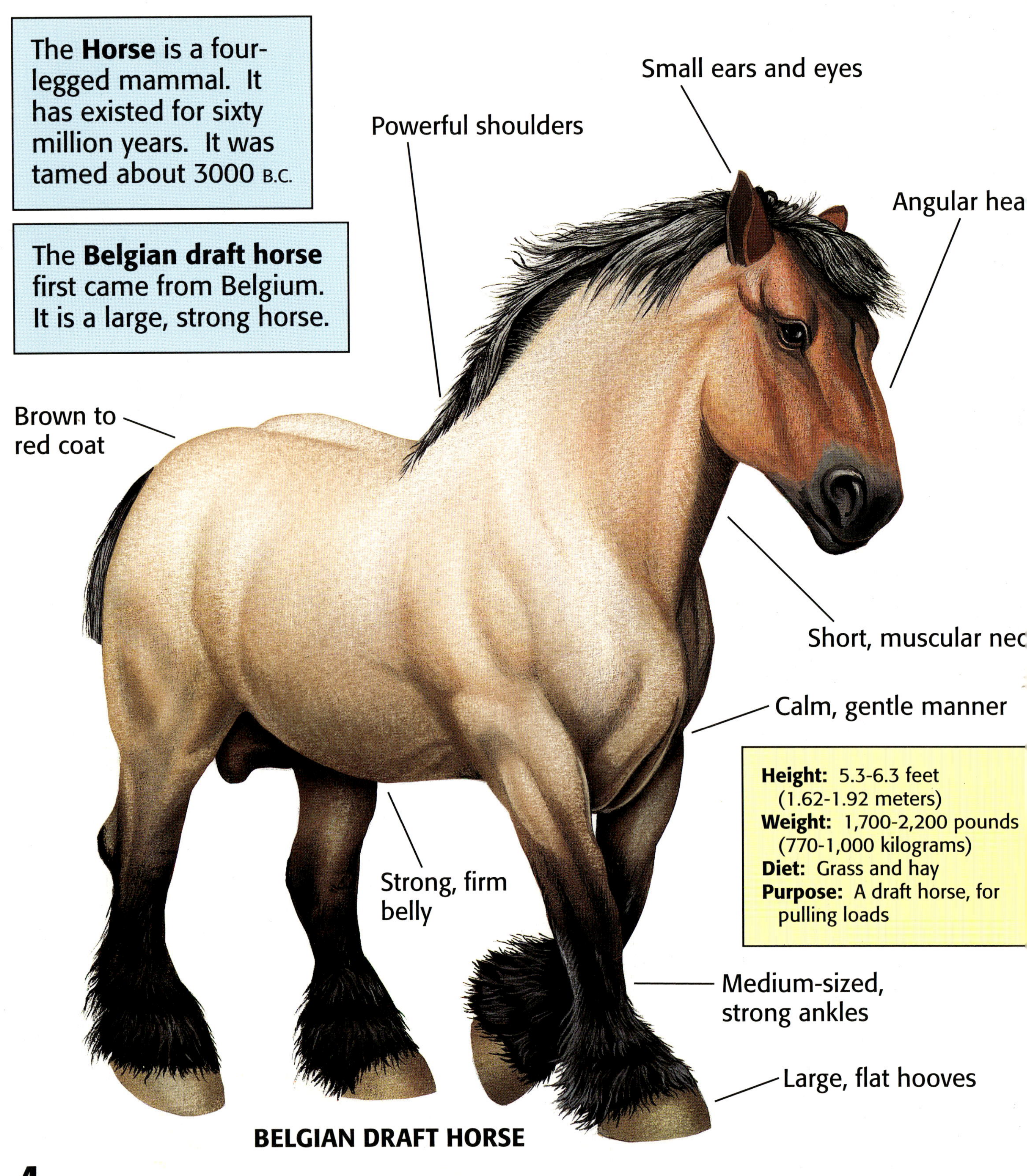

Height: 5.3-6.3 feet (1.62-1.92 meters)
Weight: 1,700-2,200 pounds (770-1,000 kilograms)
Diet: Grass and hay
Purpose: A draft horse, for pulling loads

BELGIAN DRAFT HORSE

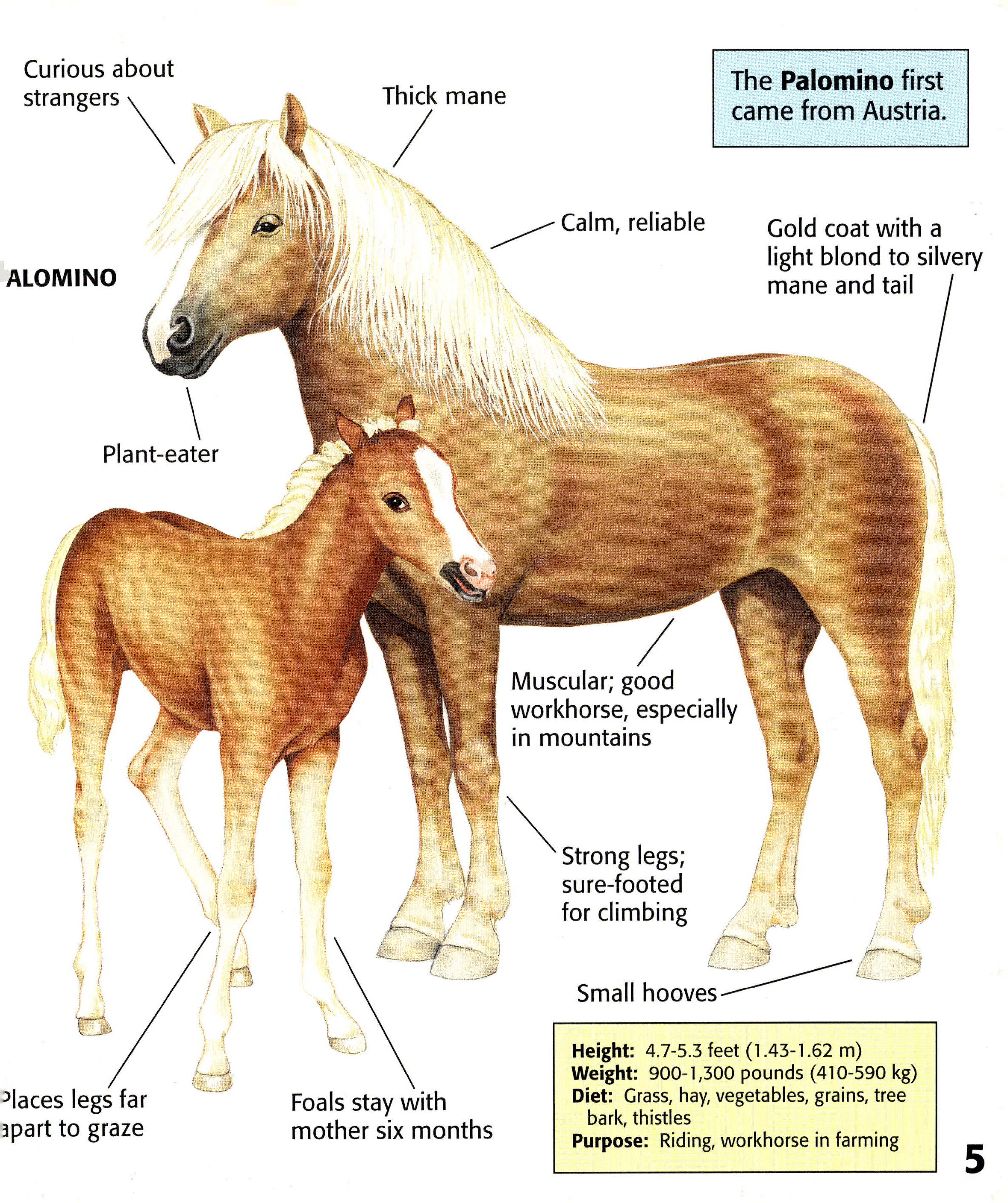

Height: 4.7-5.3 feet (1.43-1.62 m)
Weight: 900-1,300 pounds (410-590 kg)
Diet: Grass, hay, vegetables, grains, tree bark, thistles
Purpose: Riding, workhorse in farming

The **Mule** is born of a donkey (the father) and a horse (the mother). A mule is larger than a donkey.

Height: 47-67 inches (120-170 centimeters)
Weight: 600-1,545 pounds (272-700 kg)
Diet: Grass and hay
Purpose: In farming; in mining; can carry loads of almost 300 pounds (135 kg) through mountains

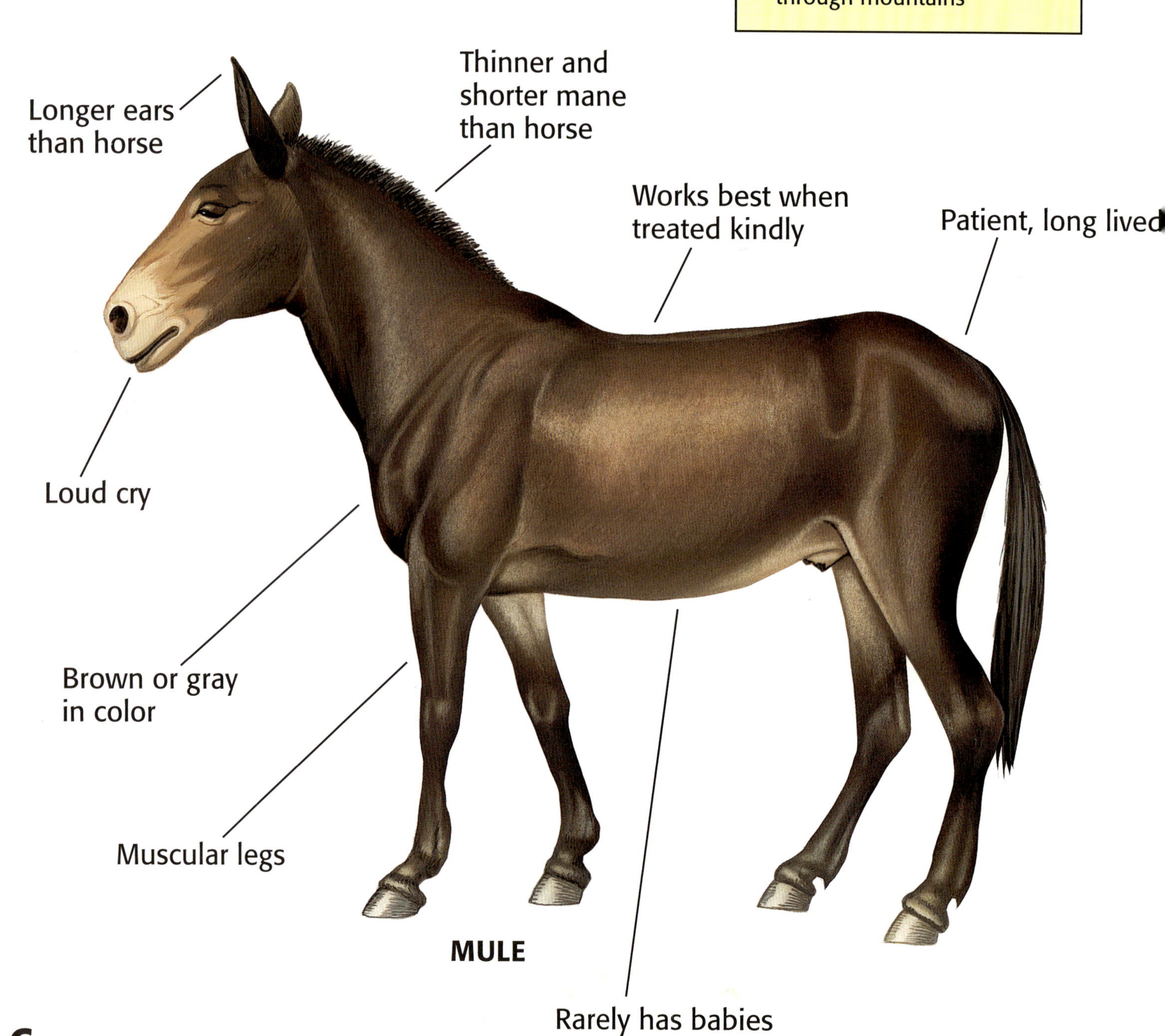

Longer ears than horse
Thinner and shorter mane than horse
Works best when treated kindly
Patient, long lived
Loud cry
Brown or gray in color
Muscular legs
Rarely has babies

MULE

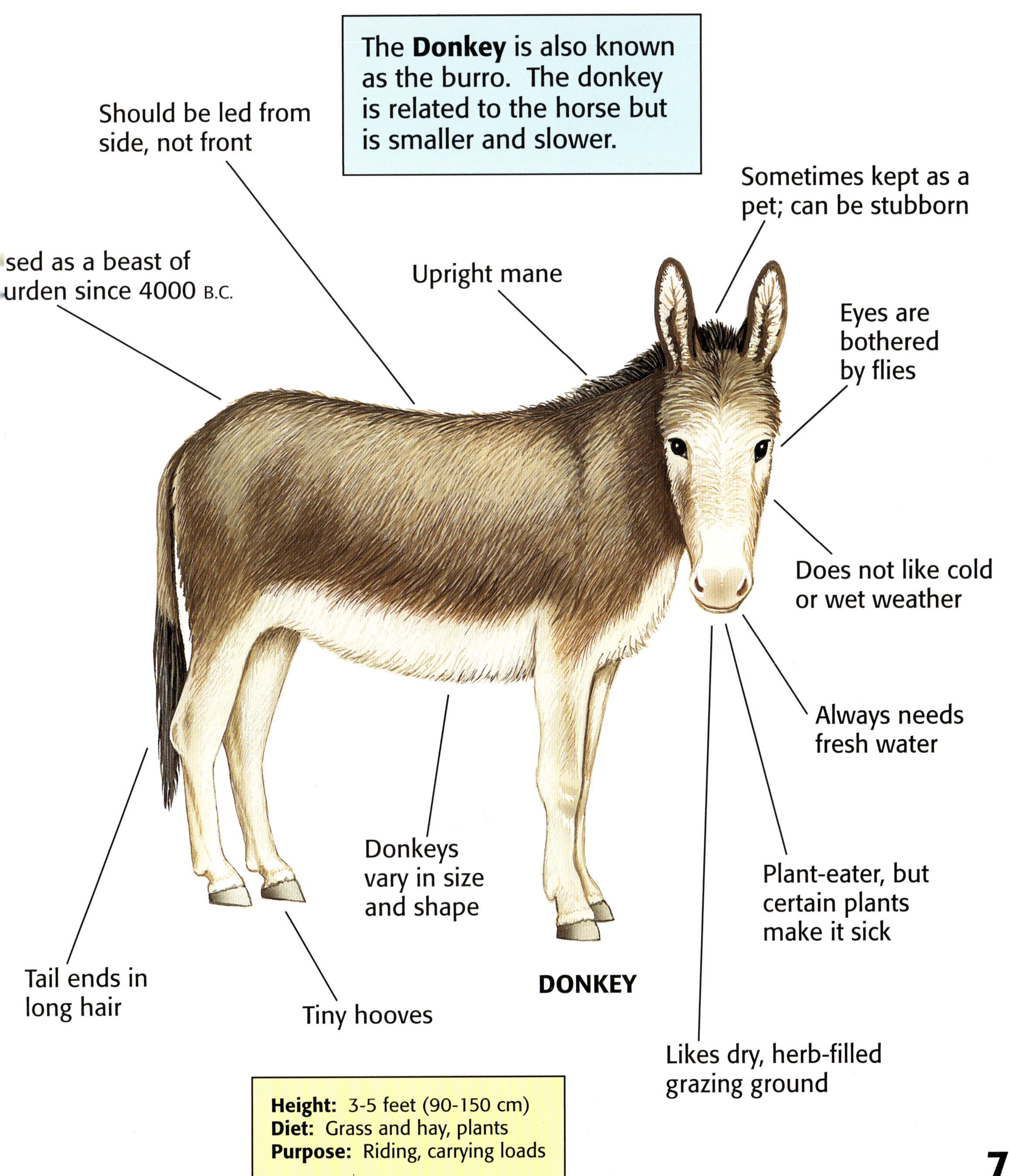
The **Donkey** is also known as the burro. The donkey is related to the horse but is smaller and slower.
Should be led from side, not front
Sometimes kept as a pet; can be stubborn
sed as a beast of urden since 4000 B.C.
Upright mane
Eyes are bothered by flies
Does not like cold or wet weather
Always needs fresh water
Donkeys vary in size and shape
Plant-eater, but certain plants make it sick
Tail ends in long hair
Tiny hooves
DONKEY
Likes dry, herb-filled grazing ground
Height: 3-5 feet (90-150 cm)
Diet: Grass and hay, plants
Purpose: Riding, carrying loads

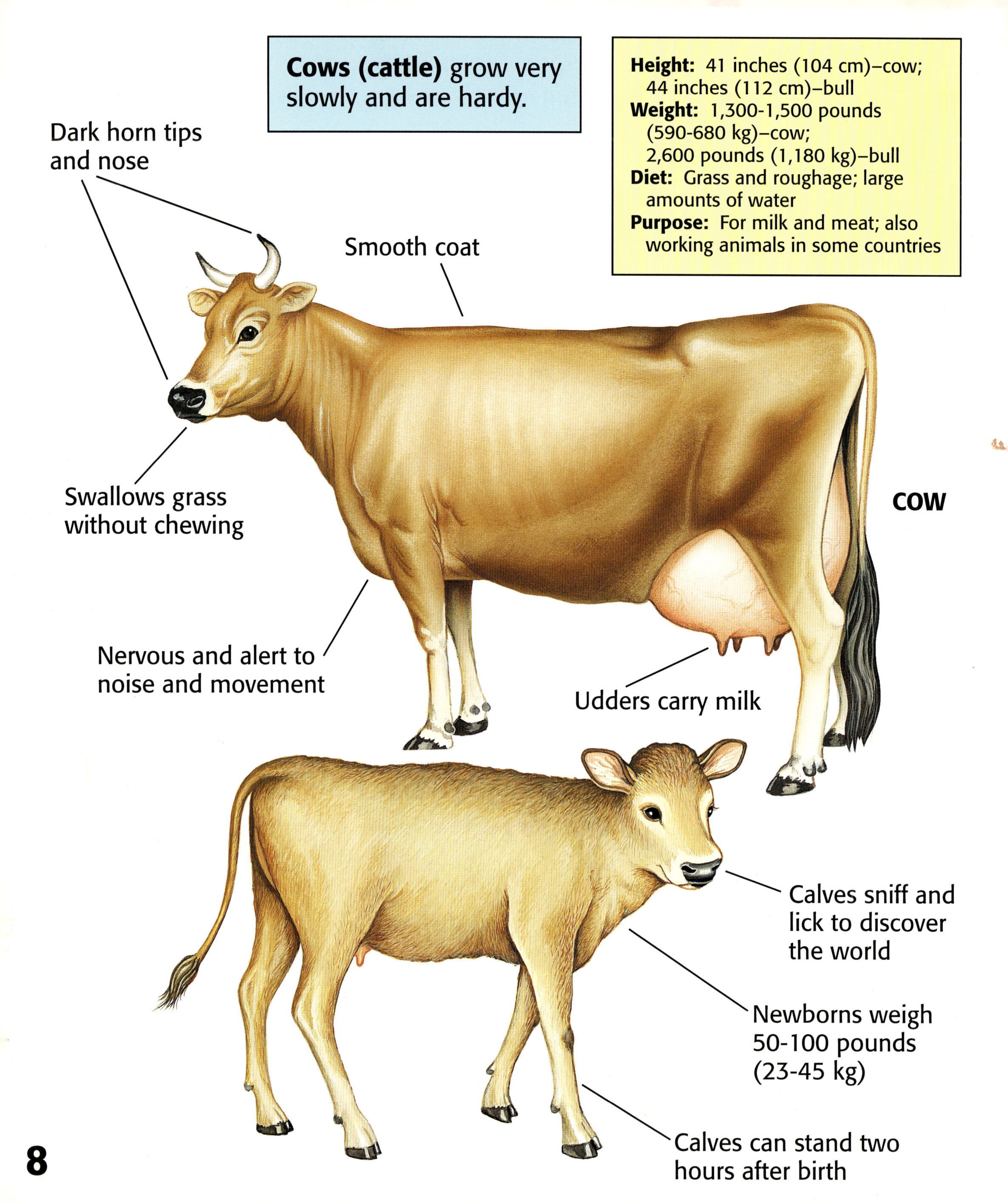
Cows (cattle) grow very slowly and are hardy.
Height: 41 inches (104 cm)–cow; 44 inches (112 cm)–bull
Weight: 1,300-1,500 pounds (590-680 kg)–cow; 2,600 pounds (1,180 kg)–bull
Diet: Grass and roughage; large amounts of water
Purpose: For milk and meat; also working animals in some countries
Dark horn tips and nose
Smooth coat
Swallows grass without chewing
COW
Nervous and alert to noise and movement
Udders carry milk
Calves sniff and lick to discover the world
Newborns weigh 50-100 pounds (23-45 kg)
Calves can stand two hours after birth

Height: 54 inches (136 cm)
Weight: 1,400-1,655 pounds (635-750 kg)–cow; 2,200-2,500 pounds (998-1,134 kg)–bull
Diet: Grass, hay
Purpose: Milk

A **Holstein** can produce about 12,500 pounds (5,670 kg) of milk each year.

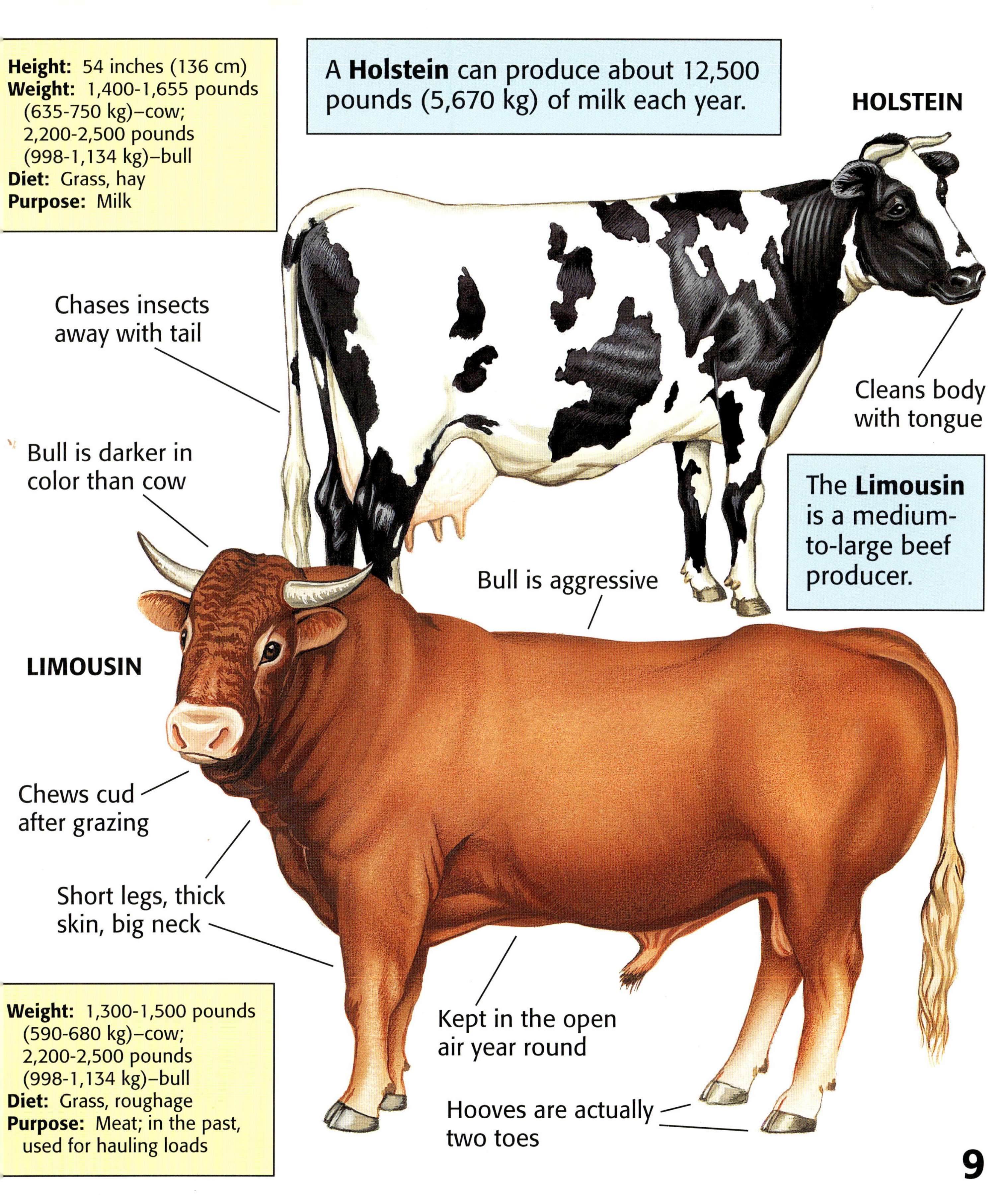

The **Limousin** is a medium-to-large beef producer.

Weight: 1,300-1,500 pounds (590-680 kg)–cow; 2,200-2,500 pounds (998-1,134 kg)–bull
Diet: Grass, roughage
Purpose: Meat; in the past, used for hauling loads

Pigs that live on farms are descended from wild pigs.

The **Hampshire** is a fast-growing pig.

Length: 30 inches (76 cm)
Weight: 500-700 pounds (227-318 kg)–sow; 600-850 pounds (272-386 kg)–boar
Diet: Barley, wheat, potatoes, corn, milk, and more
Purpose: Meat

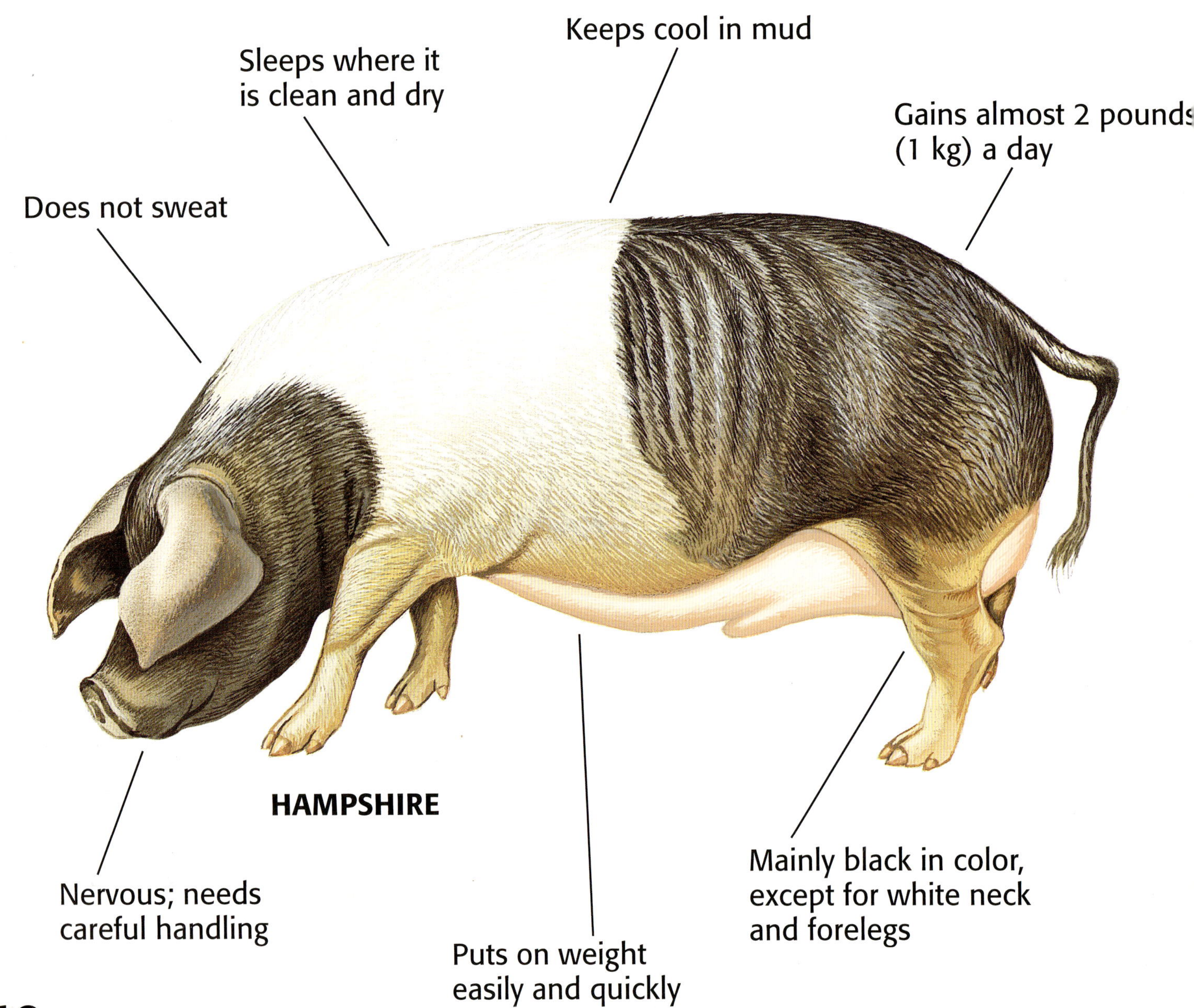
Keeps cool in mud
Sleeps where it is clean and dry
Gains almost 2 pounds (1 kg) a day
Does not sweat
HAMPSHIRE
Nervous; needs careful handling
Puts on weight easily and quickly
Mainly black in color, except for white neck and forelegs

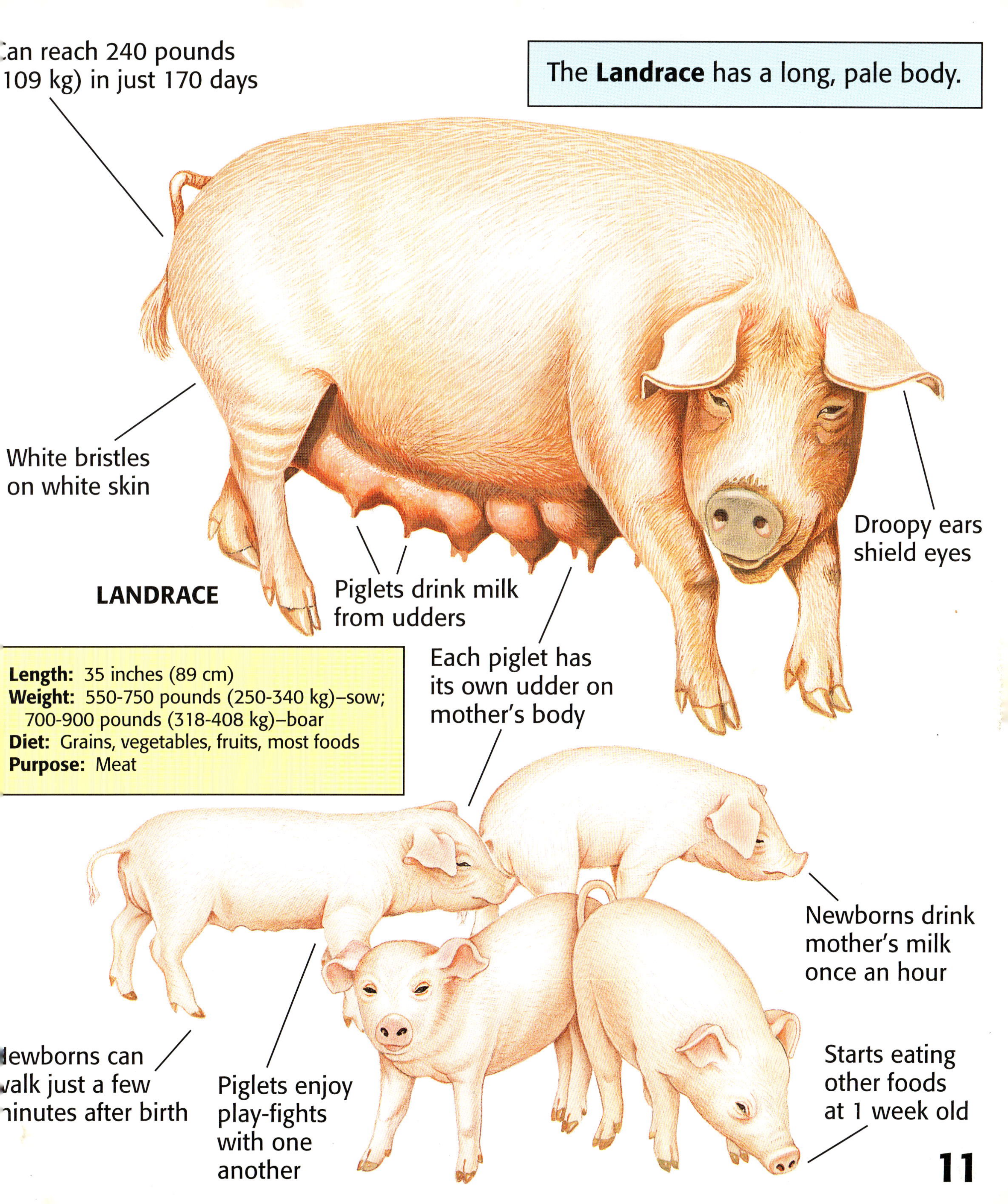
The **Landrace** has a long, pale body.
an reach 240 pounds
109 kg) in just 170 days
White bristles
on white skin
LANDRACE
Piglets drink milk
from udders
Droopy ears
shield eyes
Each piglet has
its own udder on
mother's body
Length: 35 inches (89 cm)
Weight: 550-750 pounds (250-340 kg)–sow;
700-900 pounds (318-408 kg)–boar
Diet: Grains, vegetables, fruits, most foods
Purpose: Meat
Newborns drink
mother's milk
once an hour
ewborns can
alk just a few
inutes after birth
Piglets enjoy
play-fights
with one
another
Starts eating
other foods
at 1 week old

Goats have strong horns and rough coats. They are cud chewers, storing food in their stomachs for chewing later.

The **Mountain goat** can live in steep, dry areas in which cows and sheep would not do well.

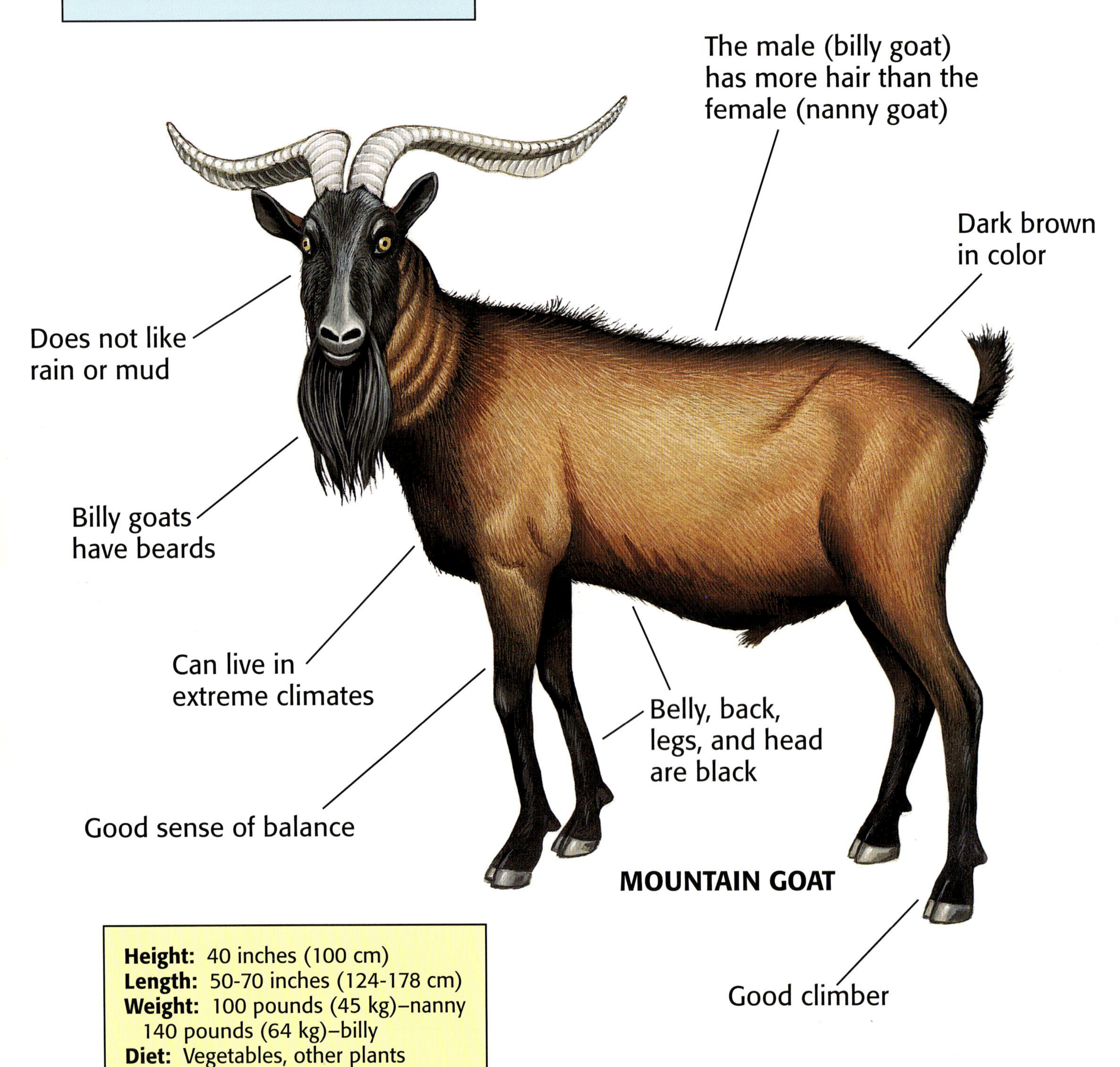
The male (billy goat) has more hair than the female (nanny goat)
Dark brown in color
Does not like rain or mud
Billy goats have beards
Can live in extreme climates
Belly, back, legs, and head are black
Good sense of balance
MOUNTAIN GOAT
Good climber

Height: 40 inches (100 cm)
Length: 50-70 inches (124-178 cm)
Weight: 100 pounds (45 kg)–nanny
140 pounds (64 kg)–billy
Diet: Vegetables, other plants
Purpose: Milk

The **Saanen goat** first came from the Saanen Valley in Switzerland.
The young, or kids, nurse on mother's milk 2-3 months
Kids play-fight
Each goat herd has a leader – the oldest nanny, or female
Short hair
Eats just about anything
Vhite or cream-olored hair
Goat's milk is easier for humans to digest than cow's milk
Roams up to 12 miles (19 kilometers) a day
Good jumper
Hooves must be trimmed
Nanny has 2 kids at a time
Height: 30-35 inches (76-89 cm)
Weight: 135 pounds (61 kg)–nanny 185 pounds (84 kg)–billy
Diet: Mainly grass, herbs, vegetables
Purpose: Milk
SAANEN GOAT

Sheep were raised long before cattle, horses, pigs, or poultry. Sheep are timid and live in herds.

Diet: Grasses and other plants
Purpose: Milk, wool, meat, fur, and hide

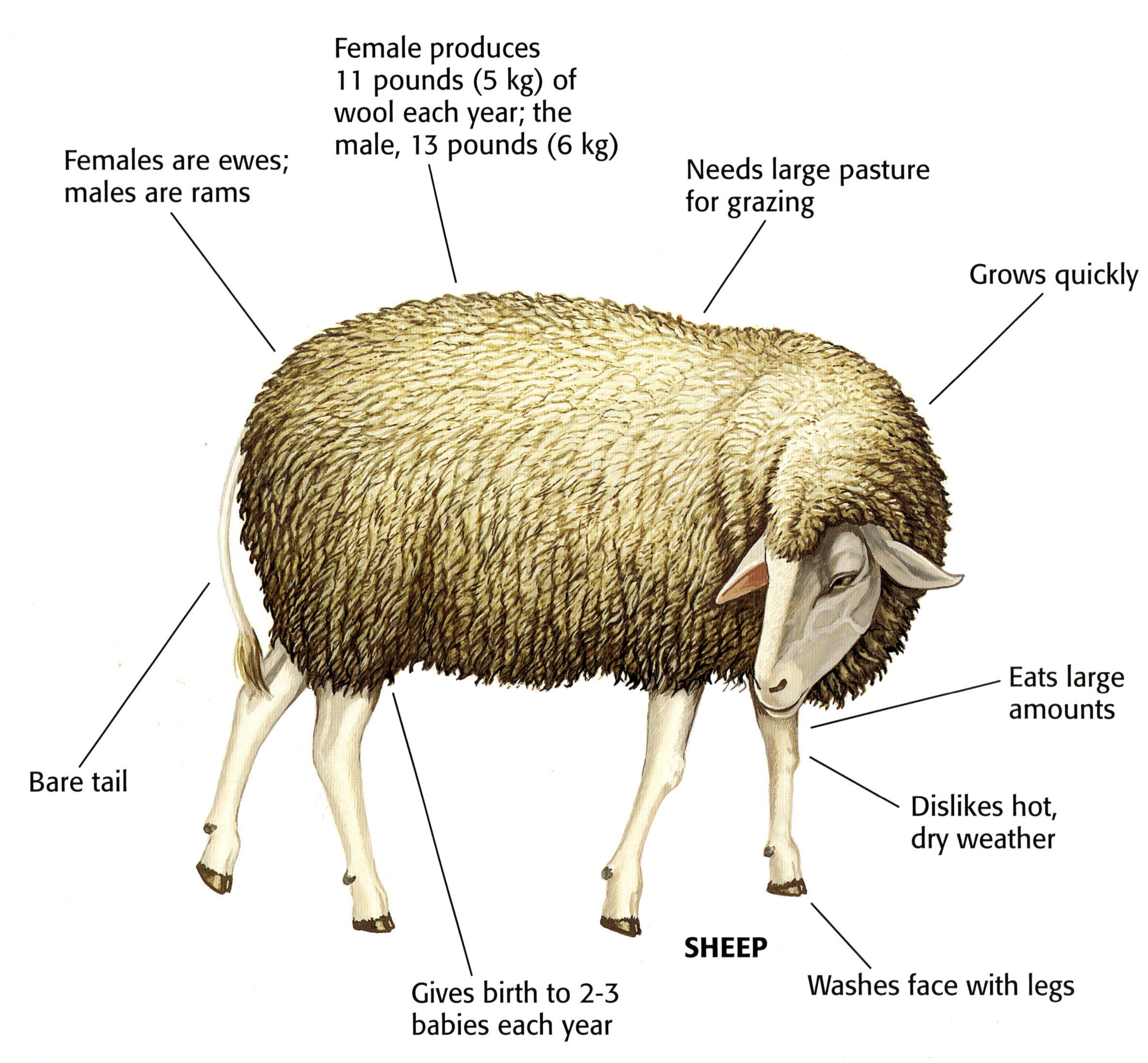

Female produces 11 pounds (5 kg) of wool each year; the male, 13 pounds (6 kg)
Females are ewes; males are rams
Needs large pasture for grazing
Grows quickly
Eats large amounts
Bare tail
Dislikes hot, dry weather
SHEEP
Gives birth to 2-3 babies each year
Washes face with legs

Weight: 50 pounds (23 kg)
Diet: Grasses and other plants
Purpose: Wool, meat, hide

The **Soay sheep** has short, tight wool.

The **North German Moorland sheep** comes in the solid colors of white, gray, or black. All have black heads and legs.

Weight: up to 190 pounds (86 kg)–ewe; up to 220 pounds (100 kg)–ram
Diet: Grasses and other plants
Purpose: Wool, meat, hide

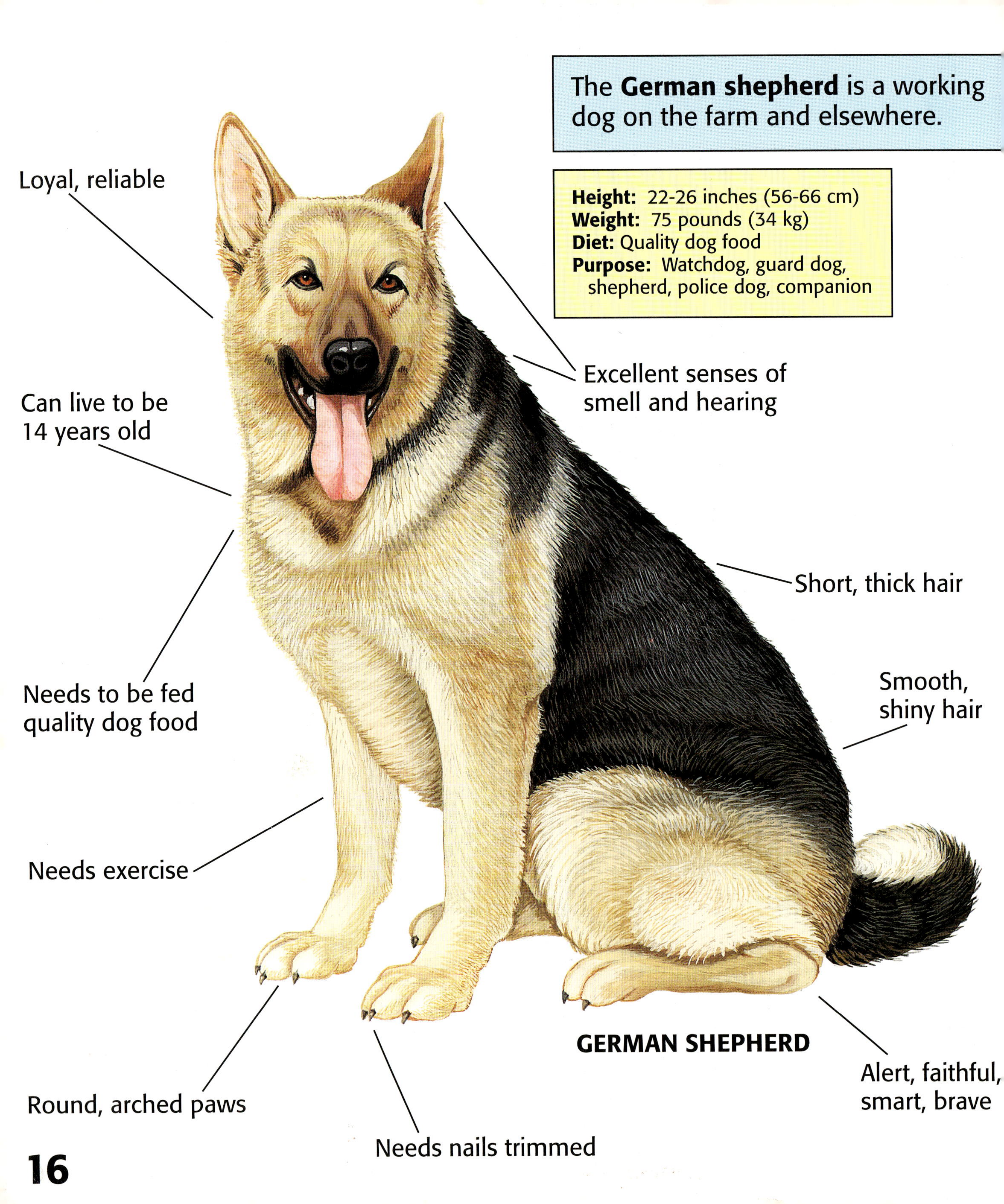
The **German shepherd** is a working dog on the farm and elsewhere.
Height: 22-26 inches (56-66 cm)
Weight: 75 pounds (34 kg)
Diet: Quality dog food
Purpose: Watchdog, guard dog, shepherd, police dog, companion
Loyal, reliable
Can live to be 14 years old
Needs to be fed quality dog food
Needs exercise
Round, arched paws
Needs nails trimmed
Excellent senses of smell and hearing
Short, thick hair
Smooth, shiny hair
Alert, faithful, smart, brave
GERMAN SHEPHERD

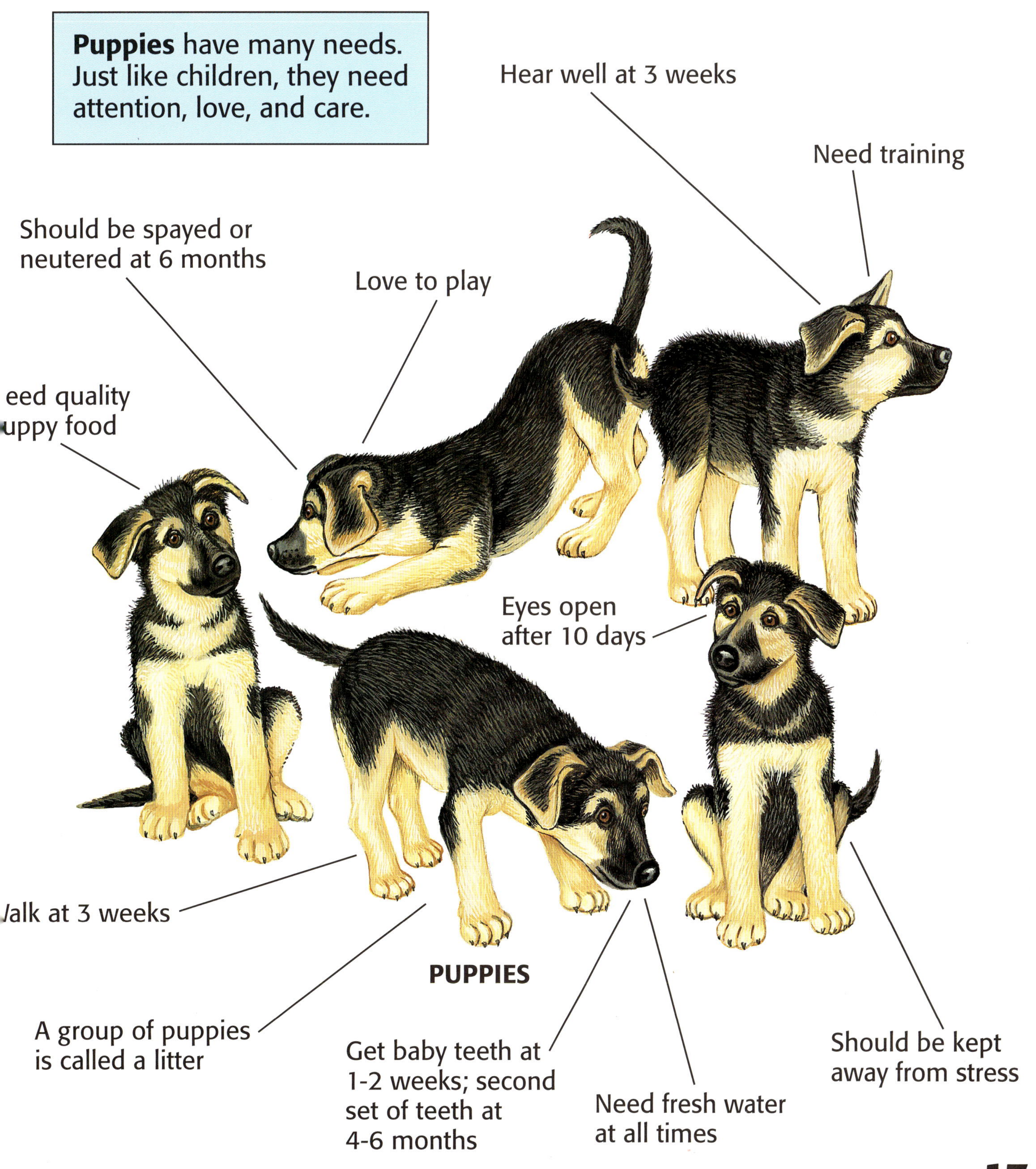
Puppies have many needs. Just like children, they need attention, love, and care.
Hear well at 3 weeks
Need training
Should be spayed or neutered at 6 months
Love to play
eed quality
uppy food
Eyes open after 10 days
alk at 3 weeks
PUPPIES
A group of puppies is called a litter
Get baby teeth at 1-2 weeks; second set of teeth at 4-6 months
Need fresh water at all times
Should be kept away from stress

Geese are web-footed birds. Tame geese on a farm can fly only short distances near the ground.
The **Toulouse goose** is the largest of the tame geese. It first came from southern France.
Weight: 17 pounds (8 kg)–female; 24 pounds (11 kg)–male
Diet: Mash, grass, corn, oats, barley, wheat
Purpose: Meat, eggs, feathers for pillows and clothing
TOULOUSE GOOSE
Good sense of hearing and sight
Gray feathers with white trim
Hisses when upset
Wide, short wings
Descendant of the wild greylag goose
Can live 30 years
Matures quickly; lays eggs when 2-5 years old
The Emden goose is a blue-eyed white bird. It first came from Germany.
EMDEN GOOSE
Weight: 20 pounds (9 kg)–female; 26 pounds (12 kg)–male
Diet: Mash, grass, corn, oats, barley, and wheat
Purpose: Meat, eggs
Webbing
Sure-footed

Ducks have been raised by humans for three thousand years.

The **Mallard** can fly very fast and high. It is much smaller than a goose.

Warm, downy coat after 10 days
Male and female are different colors
Ducklings can fly after 2 months
Swim at 1 day old
Good sense of smell
FEMALE MALLARD
Male's voice is quieter than female's
Tame females lay 50-60 eggs a year
Wide, long beak
Female chooses her mate and swims behind him, chasing away other females
Thick coat of down and layer of fat for warmth
MALE MALLARD

Length: 23 inches (58 cm)
Weight: 8-10 pounds (3.6-4.5 kg)
Diet: Grass and grains
Purpose: Meat, eggs

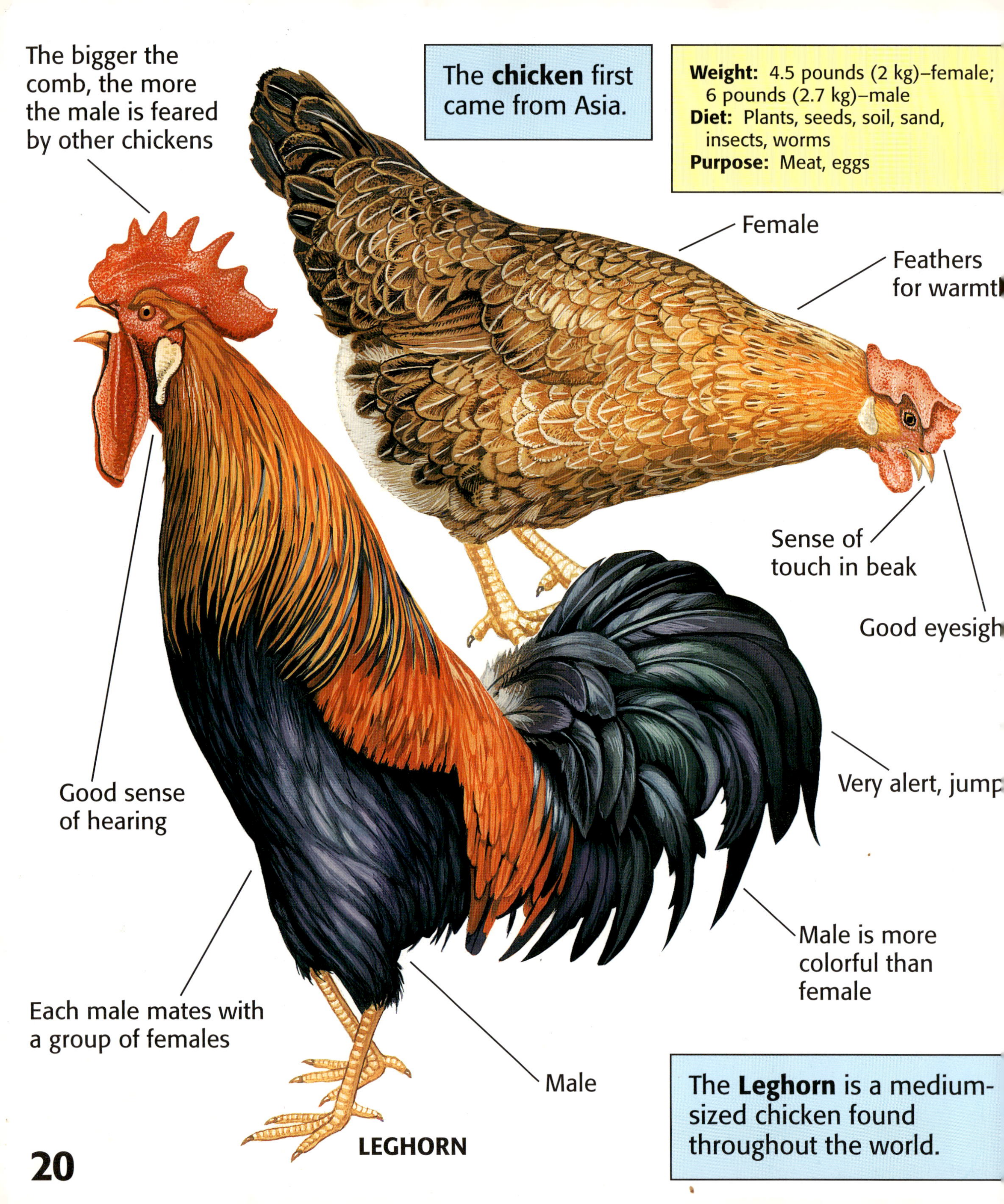
The bigger the comb, the more the male is feared by other chickens
The **chicken** first came from Asia.
Weight: 4.5 pounds (2 kg)–female; 6 pounds (2.7 kg)–male
Diet: Plants, seeds, soil, sand, insects, worms
Purpose: Meat, eggs
Female
Feathers for warmt
Sense of touch in beak
Good eyesigh
Very alert, jump
Good sense of hearing
Male is more colorful than female
Each male mates with a group of females
Male
LEGHORN
The **Leghorn** is a medium-sized chicken found throughout the world.

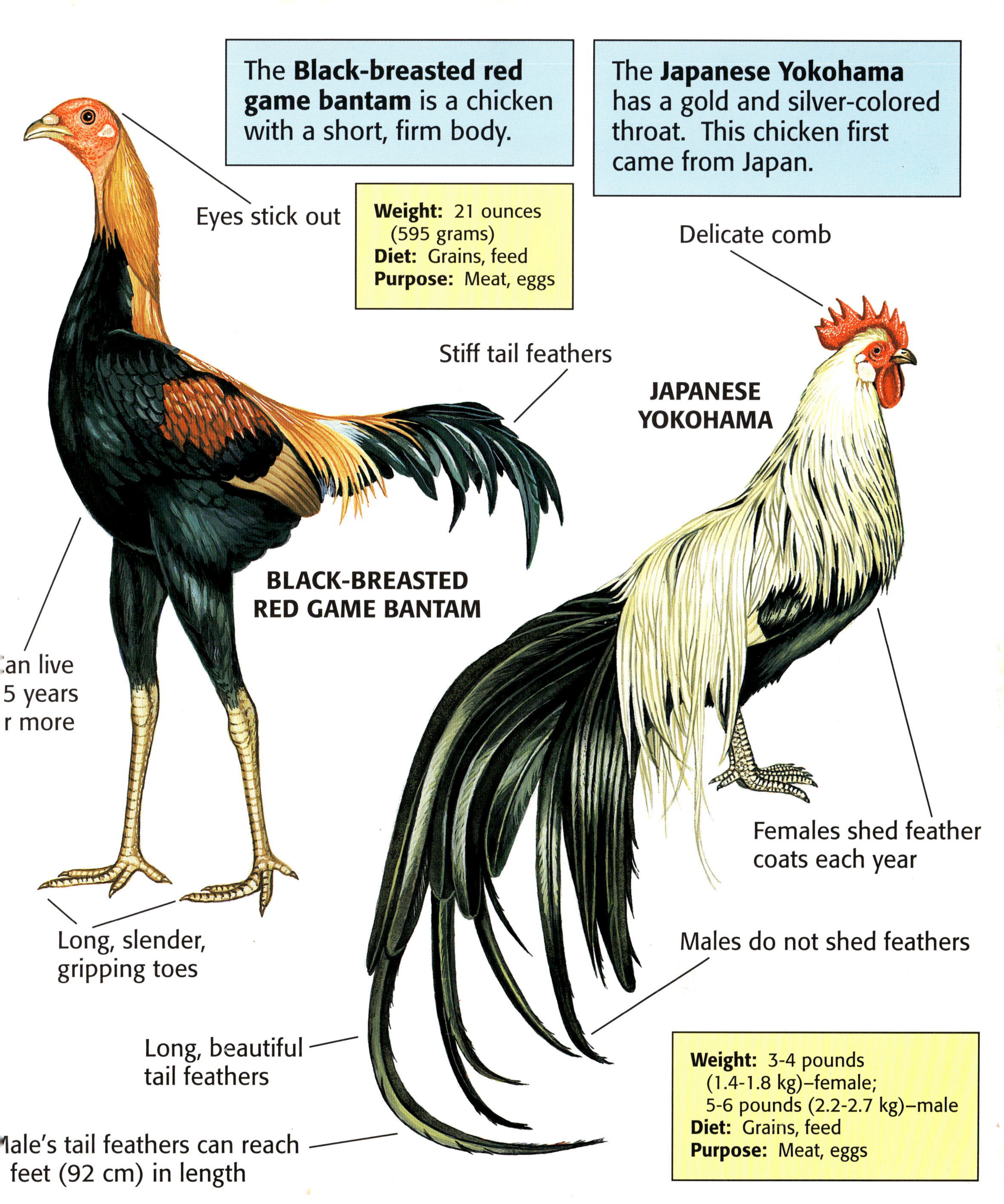

The **Black-breasted red game bantam** is a chicken with a short, firm body.
The **Japanese Yokohama** has a gold and silver-colored throat. This chicken first came from Japan.
Eyes stick out
Weight: 21 ounces (595 grams)
Diet: Grains, feed
Purpose: Meat, eggs
Delicate comb
Stiff tail feathers
JAPANESE YOKOHAMA
BLACK-BREASTED RED GAME BANTAM
an live
5 years
r more
Females shed feather coats each year
Long, slender, gripping toes
Males do not shed feathers
Long, beautiful tail feathers
ale's tail feathers can reach
feet (92 cm) in length
Weight: 3-4 pounds (1.4-1.8 kg)–female; 5-6 pounds (2.2-2.7 kg)–male
Diet: Grains, feed
Purpose: Meat, eggs

The **Turkey** first came from North, South, and Central America. It was tamed in 2500 B.C. in Mexico.

Length: 36-48 inches (91-122 cm)
Weight: 8-25 pounds (3.6-11 kg)–female; 10-30 pounds (4.5-13.6 kg)–male
Diet: Corn, oats, wheat meal, barley meal
Purpose: Meat

TURKEY

The **Guinea hen** first came from West Africa and Morocco. It has lived since prehistoric times.

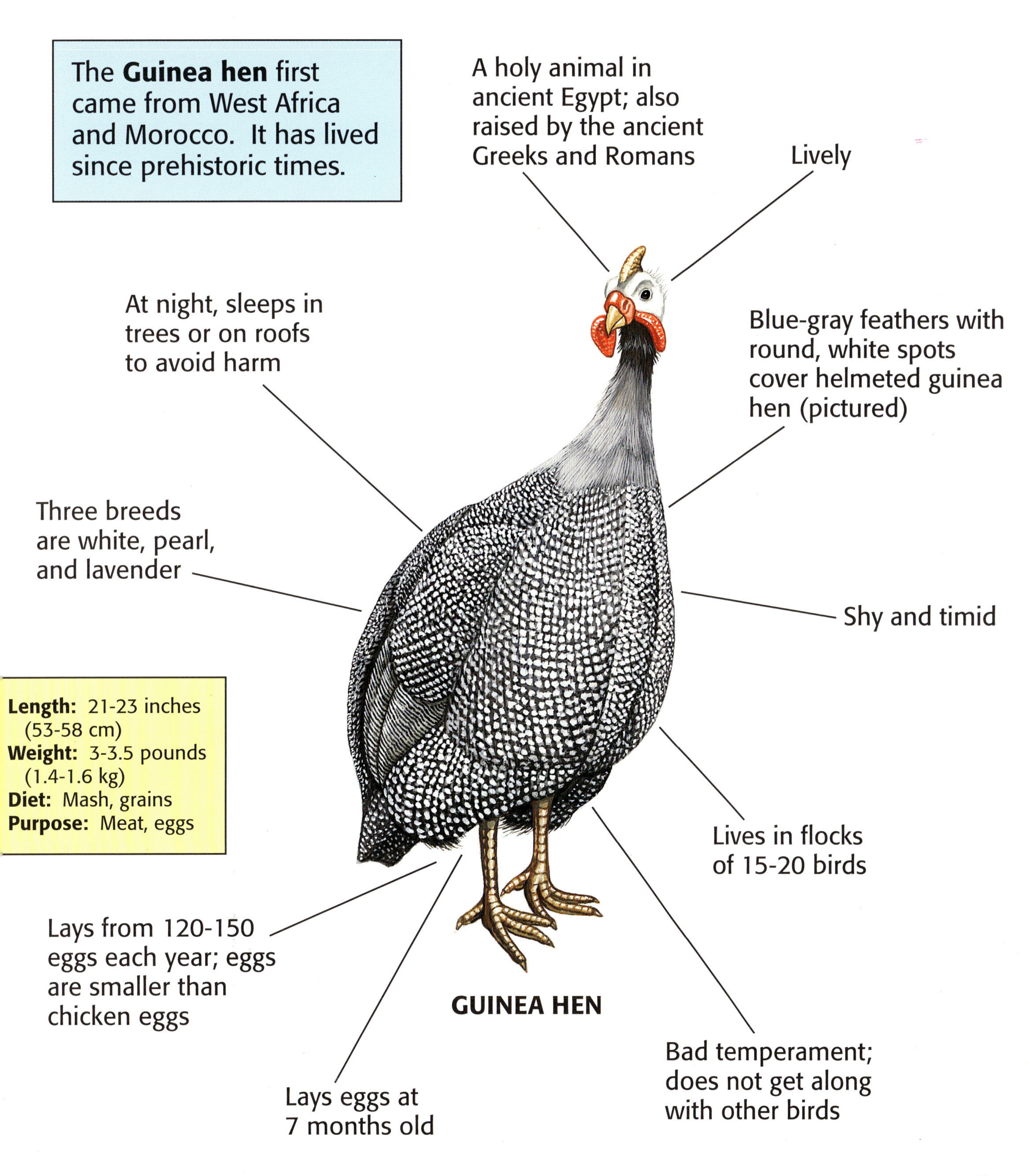
A holy animal in ancient Egypt; also raised by the ancient Greeks and Romans
Lively
At night, sleeps in trees or on roofs to avoid harm
Blue-gray feathers with round, white spots cover helmeted guinea hen (pictured)
Three breeds are white, pearl, and lavender
Shy and timid
Lives in flocks of 15-20 birds
Lays from 120-150 eggs each year; eggs are smaller than chicken eggs
GUINEA HEN
Bad temperament; does not get along with other birds
Lays eggs at 7 months old

Length: 21-23 inches (53-58 cm)
Weight: 3-3.5 pounds (1.4-1.6 kg)
Diet: Mash, grains
Purpose: Meat, eggs

Rabbits have many different kinds and colors of coats.
Droopy ears
The **Lop-eared rabbit** is short and stocky.
Weight: 4.5-6.6 pounds (2-3 kg)
Diet: Vegetables and other plants
Purpose: Pet, meat, fur
Good hearing
Good sense of smell
Grinds teeth when content
LOP-EARED RABBIT
The **German giant rabbit** is the king of all the rabbits.
Does not like to get paws or fur wet
Velvety fur
Washes its coa
every day
Weight: 11 pounds (5 kg)
Diet: Vegetables and other plants
Purpose: Pet, meat, fur
Bends down before jumping
GERMAN GIANT RABBIT
Stretches out back legs to cool o

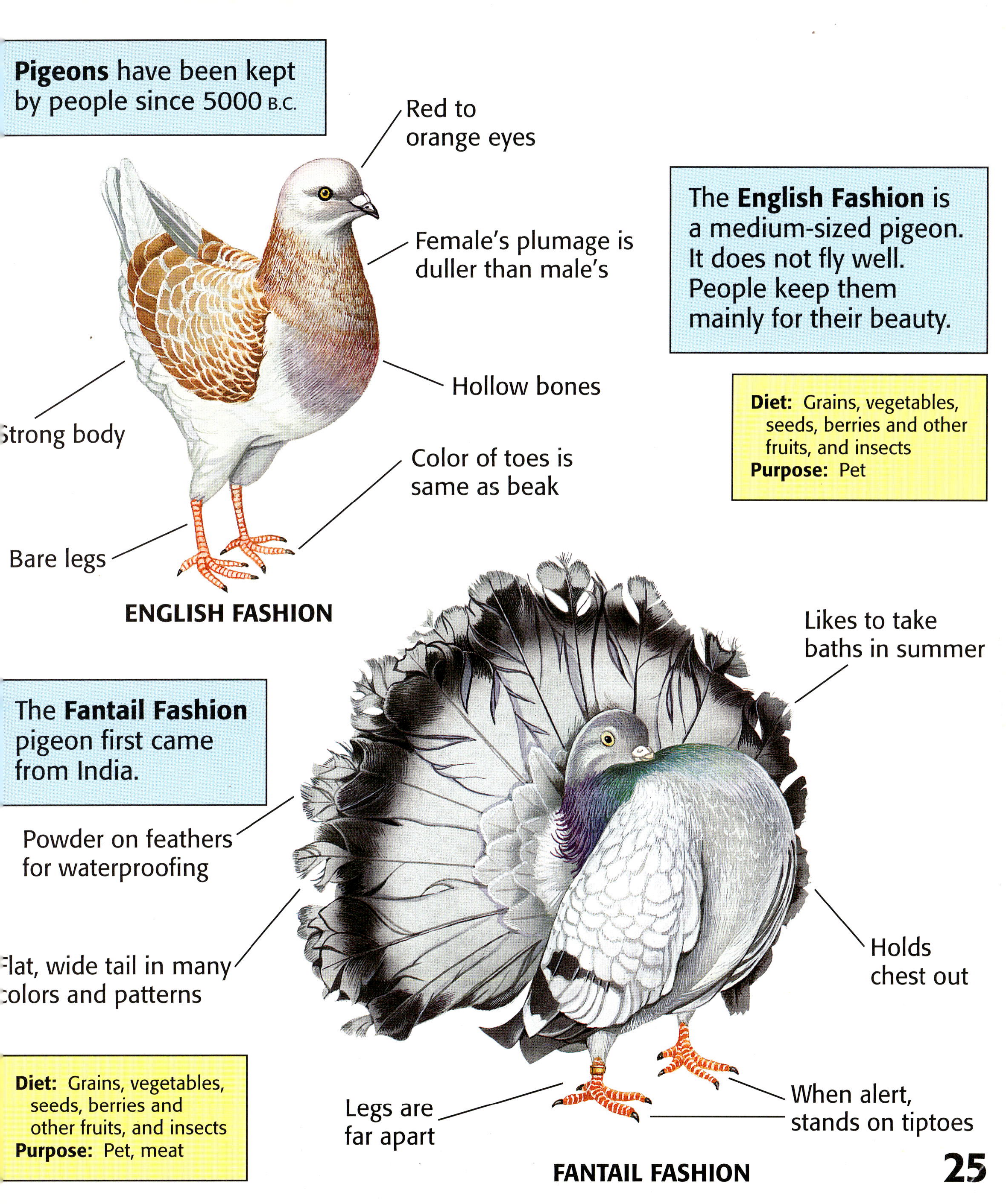

Pigeons have been kept by people since 5000 B.C.

The **English Fashion** is a medium-sized pigeon. It does not fly well. People keep them mainly for their beauty.

Diet: Grains, vegetables, seeds, berries and other fruits, and insects
Purpose: Pet

The **Fantail Fashion** pigeon first came from India.

Diet: Grains, vegetables, seeds, berries and other fruits, and insects
Purpose: Pet, meat

You would not find all the animals in this book on one farm. Each farmer keeps only certain animals depending on his or her needs and the conditions of the region in which the farm is located.

ACTIVITIES

1. Visit a petting zoo. Make a list of the animals you may find on a farm.

2. Ask your teacher or another adult to arrange a field trip to a farm. Many areas have farms set up just for this purpose. A listing of farms open to visitors might be found in a state tourism book.

3. When you go to a grocery store, notice which foods come from a farm. Make a list of the products and their source. For instance, milk comes from a cow, ham comes from a pig, eggs come from a chicken, etc.

4. Visit a cheese factory and see how cow's and goat's milk are made into cheese.

5. Make real butter! If you live near a dairy farm, perhaps you can buy some whole milk straight from the farm. Skim the cream off the milk and put it in a container that has a lid. Shake the cream until you have your very own butter!

6. Go to a state or county fair. Look at the animals that you've just read about and meet the farmers who care for them.

7. Make a picture book of farm animals. Find pictures in magazines or draw pictures of your own.

8. Spend a day horseback riding at a horse farm in your area.

FUN FACTS

1. Chickens eat pebbles to help their digestion.
2. Pigs are clean and very smart.
3. Foals and calves stand within two hours after they are born.
4. Rabbits' teeth are always growing.
5. A horse's back molars keep growing throughout its life.
6. Cows have four stomachs.
7. A cow always returns to its own stall for milking.
8. Horses are very intelligent, and they can remember things.
9. Horses are frightened easily because objects appear to move very quickly to them.
10. Most animals grow a thicker coat of fur to keep them warm in winter.
11. Geese mate for life. They can live for thirty years.
12. Goat's milk is used more than cow's milk around the world.
13. Goats don't really eat everything in sight, but they like to lick and chew cans and other things to get minerals.
14. Some dogs are trained to herd sheep and cattle.
15. Mules and donkeys are very intelligent.
16. Down refers to the under feathers of geese and ducks that keep them warm.

GLOSSARY

beast of burden: an animal used by people for carrying heavy loads.

billy goat: a male goat.

comb: the brightly colored crest on the top of a bird's head.

cud: food that has already been swallowed by an animal that is brought back up into the mouth for chewing.

draft horse: a horse used for pulling heavy loads.

ewe: a female sheep.

foal: a newborn horse.

graze: to feed on grass and plants.

hay: dried grass and alfalfa used as food for animals.

herd: a group of similar animals that stays together.

hooves: the hard, protective covering of horn on the feet of certain animals, such as horses, zebra, and cattle.

litter: the offspring of a mother animal born in one delivery.

mammal: a warm-blooded animal that has a backbone and usually has hair or fur. Mammals produce milk to feed their young.

mane: the thick, protective hair on the neck of some animals, such as horses or male lions.

nanny: a female goat.

neuter: to surgically remove parts of a male animal's reproductive system.

plumage: the feathers of a bird.

prehistoric: from the time before people began to write down events that occurred.

ram: a male sheep.

shed: to lose or drop something naturally, such as when an animal loses hair or a tree loses leaves.

shorn: removed of hair or wool.

spay: to surgically remove the ovaries of a female animal so that she cannot produce offspring.

udder: the organ of a female animal, such as a cow, that consists of mammary glands and is involved in milk production.

BOOKS TO READ

Bison Magic for Kids. Todd Wilkinson (Gareth Stevens)

Cow Girl. Meridith McGregor (Walker and Co.)

Dabble the Duckling. Jane Burton (Random House)

Farm Babies. Ann Rice (Grosset and Dunlap)

A First Look at Horses. Millicent E. Selsam/Joyce Hunt (Walker and Co.)

How Ducklings Grow. Diane Molleson (Scholastic)

Ice-Cream Cows and Mitten Sheep: A Book About Farm Animals. Jane Belk Moncure (American Education Publishing)

Magnificent Horses of the World (series). (Gareth Stevens)

Our Animal Friends at Maple Hill Farm. Alice Provensen (Random House)

Pigs and Peccaries. Animal Families. Annemarie Schmidt/Christian R. Schmidt (Gareth Stevens)

Rabbits and Hares. Animal Families. Annette Barkhausen/Franz Geiser (Gareth Stevens)

Real Baby Animals (series). (Gareth Stevens)

The Saddle Club (series). Bonnie Bryant (Gareth Stevens)

See How They Grow - Calf. Mary Ling (Dorling Kindersley)

Smart, Clean Pigs. Allan Fowler (Childrens Press)

VIDEOS

Barnyard Babies. (Grunko Films, Inc.)

Farm Animals: Up Close and Very Personal. (Stage Fright Productions)

The Milk Makers. (Lancit Media Products, Inc., Reading Rainbow)

See How They Grow – Farm Animals. (Dorling Kindersley Vision)

Spot Goes to the Farm. (Buena Vista Home Video)

PLACES TO WRITE

For more information about animals, contact the following organizations. Be sure to include a self-addressed, stamped envelope.

Canadian Wildlife Federation
2740 Queensview Drive
Ottawa, Ontario K2B 1A2

The Humane Society of the United States
2100 L Street NW
Washington, D.C. 20037

Conservation Commission of the Northern Territory
P.O. Box 496
Palmerston, NT 0831 Australia

INDEX

Belgian draft horse **4**
Black-breasted red game bantam **21**
Burro **7**

Chickens **20, 21**

Dogs **3, 16, 17, 26**
Donkey **6, 7**

Emden goose **18**
English fashion pigeon **25**

Fantail fashion pigeon **25**

Geese **18**
German giant rabbit **24**
German shepherd **16-17**
Goats **12, 13**
Greylag goose **18**
Guinea hen **23**

Hampshire pig **10**
Holstein **9**
Horses **4, 5, 6, 7**

Japanese Yokohama **21**

Landrace pig **11**
Leghorn **20**
Limousin **9**
Lop-eared rabbit **24**

Mallards **19**
Mountain goat **12**
Mule **6**

North German Moorland sheep **15**

Palomino **5**
Pigeons **25**
Pigs **10, 11**
Puppies **3, 17, 26**

Rabbits **24**

Saanen goat **13**
Sheep **14, 15**
Soay sheep **15**

Toulouse goose **18**
Turkey **22**